The Side Piece Commandments

Dick Dirkler

ISBN-13: 978-0-9911853-2-0
Library of Congress Control Number: 2018946859

DEDICATION

To all the side pieces—past, present, and future—who want to do right.

CONTENTS

INTRODUCTION

The most underappreciated position in society is the "sidepiece." For her or him, their positive contributions to the family go widely unknown and unnoticed. The "sidepiece" is an unsung hero doing a thankless job, because s/he can make marriages last. The sidepiece, although not a recipient of the benefits of a married woman, still benefits nonetheless—she is free. For her greatest gift to herself is her freedom, which allows her access to multiple resources (multiple paychecks) without "having" the responsibility of cleaning his dirty laundry, tolerating his deceit for the sake of marriage, and the constant wonder of "my man's" whereabouts, and other intruders—the type of sidepiece with the aim to destroy the family to take the man. An intruder is a selfish sidepiece better known as a "home-wrecker." A sidepiece and a home-wrecker are two different things.

Home-wreckers are selfish and deluded. Sidepieces maintain an air of self-respect, and regard for their Player and his family. She has a pleasing personality and is well-kept at all times. She, because she does not have the responsibilities of managing his children, managing him, cleaning his home, remains upbeat and worldly—she reads and is abreast of worldly events, and the events that are important to him in his world. Does she tire of her role? Does she wish for more, sometimes? Perhaps, but she is aware that this is what she has chosen. She is aware that she can get out of the situation at any time. Remember, of all the players in the game, she has the most freedom. Again, freedom is her greatest asset. Freedom remains her greatest gift to herself.

Monogamy benefits men. It does not always benefit women, until the end. Monogamy benefits poor men especially, because it makes his wife, more or less, property. It limits her freedom. Now she is only allowed to give her milk to one drinker. The sidepiece can allow multiple drinkers. In the end, the wife benefits when her man dies and receives his assets. The wife's other benefit is a partner to raise a family providing for her and the family. This is a challenge if he is a poor man. Socially, the wife is respected in society. She carries the namesake, as do her children. But she also bears the burden of being the wife with no days off.

On the other hand, the sidepiece's benefits are gained only during the relationship with the Player(s). Once the relationship ends (or he dies), her benefits stop that very day. She is not included in the last will and testament (normally); she is not mentioned in the obituary, she—if she is a pro—remains faceless and nameless. Her anonymity is her greatest asset, and she does not carry the burden of being placed on a mantle ALL the time, as does the wife. She is a free-agent and independent contractor; whereas, a wife is duty-bound. Yes, her freedom has a cost, but she knows everyone has a cost. Each day she gets to make a new choice. The only choice she cannot make is the choice to be a home-wrecker.

The sidepiece is known by many names (see Appendix A). She has had a place in history, and she will have a place in the future, for society depends on her contribution (as do most marriages...).

Here you, the reader, will find the commandments of being a successful sidepiece gathered from men and women across the world and around the globe.

I present to you the sidepiece commandments,

Dick Dirkler
a.k.a The Supreme Player from the Himalayas

1ST COMMANDMENT

These are the commandments for a side piece. Thou shalt obey. Follow these commandments at all times to maintain peace and your position. Above all, always remember that you are a side piece.

A side piece is defined as a person whom you are seeing on the side; hence, a side piece. We can say this even more explicitly and define the side piece as a piece of ass that you are getting on the side while you are a in a committed relationship with your main piece. A main piece is the person with whom you are in a committed relationship, marriage, partnership, or long-term situationship. But the main piece is the main piece and the side piece is the side piece. These two roles are mutually exclusive—one by definition cannot be the other.

The side piece must realize and accept the position on the side. Get it through your head that you are not the main piece and you do not have the same role nor do you have the same rights, privileges, or access as the main piece. There are certain things are reserved strictly for the main piece and other things that are strictly for the side piece. You are a side piece and by accepting this position, you must also accept the fact that you will never, ever be the main piece.

2ND COMMANDMENT

Thou shalt know your role—you are a side piece.

You should constantly remind yourself that you are the side piece. Knowing your role is critical to being a good and successful side piece. You play a supporting role—you are not the main character in this cast of players. You are an understudy who will never to get to play lead. However, even the understudy must rehearse the lines. You will get scheduled rehearsal time so that you can be just as good, if not better than the main piece. You are a cheerleader and it's your role to support the main piece. You are actually performing a good service for the health and vitality of the main relationship. Do everything that you can to stay in your lane. And when that dreadful day comes that you catch a feeling, you should center yourself, grab hold of that emotion and shake it loose. Do not even fool yourself into thinking that you are more than a side piece.

As part of your role as a side piece, you are to keep a happy and cheerful home. Your place should be an oasis and paradise where the Player can escape for rest and rejuvenation.

3RD COMMANDMENT

The main piece is a jealous lover—Thou [the side piece] will never be more important than the main piece. The main piece always comes before the side piece.

This commandment comes along with knowing your role as a side piece. The main piece will always come before the side piece. Whatever the Player has going on at their own home comes before whatever is going on at your home. In the order of priority, the main thing comes first, the children come second, and the side piece comes fourth or fifth. But do know that you, the side piece, will get taken care of as soon possible. Don't be anxious. Don't blow up the Player's phone or texting device with multiple calls. I promise you will get a response—it may take a day or two but you will get a response. If something is wrong with your car, call a mechanic. If something is wrong with the plumbing in your house, call a plumber. It the sinks backs up, the toilet won't stop running, or stove won't work, call a maintenance man. The Player is there for one reason—to get some pussy and ass or dick. Of course mutual benefits can come along with the package deal but your role is always secondary. You are secondary to the wife, kids, family, and work.

4TH COMMANDMENT

**Thou shalt keep your emotions to yourself.
A side piece should be
happy, cheerful, and drama-free.**

A side piece should not cause any drama. In fact, the side piece is where the Player goes to escape drama. Therefore, you should not ever cause any drama. Find ways to minimize stress. Learn how to do massage therapy and bedroom tricks. Blow the Players mind every time they arrive at your place. Figure out what upsets the Player and avoid those things at all

7

cost. Be happy and cheerful. Laugh to keep the mood light and don't ever drop too many serious questions. The Player did not come to be interrogated nor respond to a legal deposition. The Player did not come to philosophize on grand theories about the day, but instead, the Player came to play. Be playful and upbeat so that the dick can be rode in peace or that pussy be banged like a snare drum. The last thing the Player wants to do is visit the side piece and have to endure more drama and nagging. The Player can get that at home. Make your side piece relationship special.

We are not suggesting that you turn yourself into an emotionless, manic robot with a never-ending smile. At the very least, the point here is to be drama-free.

In that same regard, Thou shalt always have a pleasing personality. You, the side piece, is the

Player's source of relief. You should be a walk on the beach; a cool breeze on a hot summer's night. You are something that I, the Player, cannot have all the time of my responsibilities but when I do, make me say, "I got to do this more often...!" You should be like a warm fireplace after walking inside from the cold monotony of the snowstorm of a life that is brutal, family, work, and home. The priorities for the Player are family, work, and home, family, work, and home, occasionally the fellas, and most occasionally, you. You are my dessert—too much of together would not be a good. Too much of you, although delicious, would be bad for me. You do care about my health, don't you? If so, then you will understand that you are an integral part of making my marriage work successfully. You help me and my wife stay together—always remember that. Never be the reason that my marriage falls apart. For if you do, then I will never forgive you and you will never see me. You won't end up with me. I won't end up with you. You will not exist to me anymore. Matter of fact, you may not exist (just joking).

5TH COMMANDMENT

Thou shall be flexible with your time.

The side piece must be flexible with your time. The Player has to work and tend to home first, then the Player can find time for you. This may mean that the Player will call you or visit you during random hours—sometimes late at night, sometimes early in the morning, sometimes in the middle of the day. You just need to be ready and available.

6ᵀᴴ COMMANDMENT

Thou shalt never call the Player's home.

Under no circumstance, even if you fear that I have been hurt, maimed, lamed, injured, wounded, or even worse, died—DO NOT CALL THE PLAYER'S HOME. House calls, house visits, hospital calls, "my mama house" calls are strictly prohibited. Call to Jesus if you are looking for me. DO NOT UNDER ANY CIRCUMSTANCE CALL HOMEBASE. This is grounds for dismissal of our situationship. In fact, it is an automatic violation of Appendix 2 of the Side Piece

Contract, and therefore, warrant an automatic

termination.

7TH COMMANDMENT

The side piece has designated times to call and/or text.

Everyone is familiar with the universal booty call hours. Booty call hours are between 11:00 PM and 3:00 AM. Most decent restaurants close their grill at 11:00 PM, so if you get a call at this hour, it's definitely not to grab a meal. Most movie theaters have a last showing at midnight and it's highly doubtful that you are getting a call at this time of hour to go see a matinee movie. But a booty call can come at ANY hour of the day—8:30 AM on the way to work or 11:30 AM on lunch break, or 2:15 PM on the way to pick the kids up from school. Be ye ready—that's in the Bible. Stay ready and keep it ready—fresh and clean.

8TH COMMANDMENT

Thou shalt not call my phone with no bullshit. Thou shall not complain.

Just don't do it—don't call my phone with no bullshit!

And I do mean, no kind of bullshit. Your heartache

cannot be my headache. Yes, there will be times

where I am unavailable for whatever reason at any

given time, but please, please do NOT call me with no

bullshit. Don't be worried, concerned, pissed, nor

angry. Be pleasant. A good side piece does not

complain. You accept what you get and don't make a fuss about it. The side piece should must constantly remind themselves that this situation is only for the benefits. If at any point, the benefits don't equal investment, then the easiest thing to do is seek a mutual termination. Things can go horribly wrong if the termination is not executed properly. There should be no love lost if the side piece or the Player terminates the side piece agreement. There are more side pieces in the sea. One can get attached to a good side piece. A good pipelayer or a good piece of pie can be addictive. There will be a natural tendency to want it whenever you want it; however, that is not always possible. So don't complain, just be flexible and get it whenever you can get it.

9TH COMMANDMENT

Honor thy side piece at least one day out of the year but not on Valentine's Day, not on Sweetest Day, and definitely not Christmas—the Side Piece Valentine's Day shall be February 15th and Christmas shall be December 26th.

The side piece does not celebrate the regular holiday. Valentine's Day is February 14th. The side piece Valentine's Day is February 15th. Sweetest Day is not a global holiday—expect no gift for Sweetest Day. Christmas for the side piece is December 26th. The main day that the holiday falls on is reserved for the main piece and the kids. Do not expect a visit nor a call. Do you on these days and tend to your regularly scheduled business. The side piece will be honored, just not on the main day. And if your birthday falls on a day that the main thing has an event, then your birthday will be celebrated at the next earliest day that is convenient. Be flexible, you will get your day. Matter of fact, I officially decree February 15th as "Side Piece Day"! Don't text the Player phone with any sad face emojis, "I miss you's,"—NOTHING on Valentine's Day nor Christmas Day. Do not bring that shit to me in anyway—the player is officially OCCUPIED.

Just remember that your birthday is yours so long as it does not fall on the wife or the children's day or any other major family day. Your day means the world to the Player. I am thankful that your mother and father conceived you—they bore a side piece. The Player will be there for you on most any other day that doesn't fall on a family day.

10TH COMMANDMENT

The side piece shall never acknowledge the Player in public if they are with the main piece.

We have a private relationship. Out in public, we do not exist. Do not under any circumstance acknowledge or approach the Player in public if they are with the main piece; and especially if they are with the children. There are permanent boundaries to the side piece relationship. The side piece and the Player should not be seen in public together. Don't ever ask for public meetings; especially in the same city. However, on the rare occasion that we do meet in public, we will never arrive together and we will never leave together. We never act like we are familiar—I don't know you and you don't know me. The side piece should step in line with the social situation. Don't ever think that public displays of affection are ever appropriate—there will be no holding hands, no kissing, and no touching in front of open windows or open doors. Do not expect walks in the park or any lovey-dovey activity.

11TH COMMANDMENT

Thou shalt not get the side piece pregnant.

Do not get the side piece pregnant. Under no circumstance shall you get the side piece pregnant. This will cause drama—guaranteed drama. For if the side piece becomes pregnant, then she takes on a whole new role—The Baby Mama. Baby Mama Drama can be way more depressing and disruptive than any side piece drama. Do everything in your power to make sure that a pregnancy does not occur.

Utilize the proper birth control and always, always use condoms to prevent the transmission of sexual diseases. You don't ever want to catch something from the side piece and give it the main piece--this will break up a happy home. Every now and again, the Player needs a reminder too that the side piece is not the main thing. Children are only for the main piece. In the rare case that the side piece does become pregnant, prepare your heart and your home for the new bundle of joy. The child will be innocent and have no knowledge of the broken side piece commandment. Support the side piece throughout the entire pregnancy and love the kid with all your heart. The side piece must still realize that they are a side piece and still have no priority over the main piece. And during this time, the main piece may require some distance—just ride the wave and renegotiate the terms of the side piece agreement once you become the Baby Mama. To avoid all of this, do not get the side piece pregnant. Somewhere in the Bible, around the Book of Genesis, it tells us that a side piece got pregnant and that started a thousand year war that is still being waged today (Remember Abraham, Sarah, and Isaac and Hagar and Ishmael). Help save the world and just don't do it!

12TH COMMANDMENT

Thou shalt not get caught. Never bring the side piece to your house and the side piece should never send any gifts by delivery.

Player's do all that you can to not get caught. Don't ever, ever, ever tell your wife or main piece about your side piece. On what planet does that ever make sense? Nothing good can come of the main piece knowing about the side piece. Never take your side piece to your house. Should that ever happen, the side piece will be able to describe everything in your house in the event that s/he wants to be messy and contact the main piece.

The side piece should never send any gifts, any food, ANY thing to you at your home or your office—there is no dropping shit off. Don't send no shit nowhere—the Player will drop by and pick up anything that needs to retrieved.

Don't communicate with the side piece in front of anyone, especially the kids. The kids listen when you think they aren't. They are aware when you talk low, when you think they're sleep, they don't be. They are sensitive to your tone and will tell mommy dearest everything. Above all, the kids should not ever meet the side piece. Don't have the kids in the car when you go by or "drop by" on the side piece—they have perfect memories and will say to there mother, "This is the way Daddy drove when we went to visit that lady." The kids have a sixth sense when some hanky-panky going on—just avoid contact.

In the event that you do see your side piece at church (although you never will), treat her like every other holy sister in the place. If you holy hug every holy sister in the place, holy hug your side piece. If you say, "Hi Holy Sister," to every holy sister in the place, then you say, "Hi Holy Sister," to your side piece. If you treat her any different, that will the be sign to your main piece that something is going on. Let not the fruits of your spirit be seen in church.

Make sure that the side piece is not a friend of your wife, girlfriend, or main piece. Having a side piece that is a friend of your main piece is a recipe of disaster. Even a dog won't shit where he sleeps. This is one of the greatest infringements of the side piece commandments. Think about it, a friend of the wife has access to you. Don't even look at them. Talk to them out the side of your neck. Speak and keep it moving. Every bell and whistle in your head should say, "Danger! Danger! Danger!" The minute that she gets mad, she will throw shade and stew poison and that's all she wrote. Bye, bye life. Bye, bye, wife. Bye, bye family. You have just fucked up.

13TH COMMANDMENT

Never bring the side piece to the main piece home.

The side piece should not even know where the Player lives. This saves unnecessary drama. The side piece should not ever get angry and potentially show up the home where the main piece lives. This will result in an immediate termination of the side piece agreement. Meet the side piece at the side piece home or at a private location far away from the main piece.

14TH COMMANDMENT

The side piece shall have no rights—all benefits end with the termination of the side piece agreement.

The side piece has no rights. Let's be clear—you can be the side piece for twenty years and you still have no rights. If the Player dies tomorrow, don't show up to the funeral as if you hold a special place. No, all benefits end when the side piece agreement ends. Matter of fact, don't even show up to the funeral—

mourn in private. Every benefit you should have received was given while the side piece agreement was in effect. Expect no acknowledgment for the role that you played. You will not be thanked for your contribution—the side piece position is a thankless role. You get it while you can and move on after it's all done.

15TH COMMANDMENT

Obey the side piece commandments.

Follow the side piece commandments with all your heart, your mind, and your spirit. Do not deviate one inch from these side piece commandments. A happy main piece and a happy side piece equal a happy life. The days of your life shall be long and joyous if you follow these commandments and short and stressful if you do not.

THE SIDE PIECE AGREEMENT

Under no circumstances will you actually sign this agreement!

I, _____, (Your Name), with sound mind and body, knowingly agree and consent to be a side piece. I understand that I am a side piece and no rights or benefits other than some consensual dick, pussy, or ass. I, the side piece, will not catch feelings nor cause any drama. I will not become crazy, act crazy, or do anything crazy. I know my place and my role. I, the side piece, know that that main thing always takes priority over me. I, the side piece, will do all that I can be cheerful, happy, and drama-free. I am a side piece and will do all that I can to make the Player happy. I, the side piece, acknowledge that I can be terminated at any time, for any reason, without warning and I will be okay with that because I am a side piece. I will be available as needed. Signed in your heart, The Side Piece.

THE SIDE PIECE AGREEMENT

Under no circumstances will you actually sign this agreement!

I, _____, (Your Name), with sound mind and body, knowingly agree and consent to be a side piece. I understand that I am a side piece and no rights or benefits other than some consensual dick, pussy, or ass. I, the side piece, will not catch feelings nor cause any drama. I will not become crazy, act crazy, or do anything crazy. I know my place and my role. I, the side piece, know that that main thing always takes priority over me. I, the side piece, will do all that I can be cheerful, happy, and drama-free. I am a side piece and will do all that I can to make the Player happy. I, the side piece, acknowledge that I can be terminated at any time, for any reason, without warning and I will be okay with that because I am a side piece. I will be available as needed. Signed in your heart, The Side Piece.

THE SIDE PIECE AGREEMENT

Under no circumstances will you actually sign this agreement!

I, _____, (Your Name), with sound mind and body, knowingly agree and consent to be a side piece. I understand that I am a side piece and no rights or benefits other than some consensual dick, pussy, or ass. I, the side piece, will not catch feelings nor cause any drama. I will not become crazy, act crazy, or do anything crazy. I know my place and my role. I, the side piece, know that that main thing always takes priority over me. I, the side piece, will do all that I can be cheerful, happy, and drama-free. I am a side piece and will do all that I can to make the Player happy. I, the side piece, acknowledge that I can be terminated at any time, for any reason, without warning and I will be okay with that because I am a side piece. I will be available as needed. Signed in your heart, The Side Piece.

THE SIDE PIECE AGREEMENT

Under no circumstances will you actually sign this agreement!

I, _____, (Your Name), with sound mind and body, knowingly agree and consent to be a side piece. I understand that I am a side piece and no rights or benefits other than some consensual dick, pussy, or ass. I, the side piece, will not catch feelings nor cause any drama. I will not become crazy, act crazy, or do anything crazy. I know my place and my role. I, the side piece, know that that main thing always takes priority over me. I, the side piece, will do all that I can be cheerful, happy, and drama-free. I am a side piece and will do all that I can to make the Player happy. I, the side piece, acknowledge that I can be terminated at any time, for any reason, without warning and I will be okay with that because I am a side piece. I will be available as needed. Signed in your heart, The Side Piece.

THE SIDE PIECE AGREEMENT

Under no circumstances will you actually sign this agreement!

I, _____, (Your Name), with sound mind and body, knowingly agree and consent to be a side piece. I understand that I am a side piece and no rights or benefits other than some consensual dick, pussy, or ass. I, the side piece, will not catch feelings nor cause any drama. I will not become crazy, act crazy, or do anything crazy. I know my place and my role. I, the side piece, know that that main thing always takes priority over me. I, the side piece, will do all that I can be cheerful, happy, and drama-free. I am a side piece and will do all that I can to make the Player happy. I, the side piece, acknowledge that I can be terminated at any time, for any reason, without warning and I will be okay with that because I am a side piece. I will be available as needed. Signed in your heart, The Side Piece.

APPENDIX A
List of Common Side Piece Names

Gigolo
Geisha
Courtesan
Concubine
Mistress
Kept Woman
Lover
Paramour
Companion
Polyamorous
Polygamy
Harlot
Squeeze
Boo
Whore
Hoe
Thot
Informal Lady
Girlfriend
Boyfriend
Bit on the Side

ABOUT THE AUTHOR

Dick Dirkler is an internationally renowned male gigolo. He has been a gigaloo spanning over four decades. Dick made it through the 90's and 00's with many side pieces—a total that could rival only NBA basketballer Wilt Chamberlain. Dick is known around the world as the "Player from the Himalayas"! He held this title consecutive years in a row.